Apart from Our

Own
Reflections

A. R. Fisher

For Sandy

Chapter 1

The hallway was silent except for the footsteps behind me. The power had gone out and I was on my way back from the restroom. The footsteps came faster and lighter, then slowed and stopped. I turned around a saw a classroom door open. I turned back to the way I was heading.

"Hiya buddy."

"Holy jeez Penny," I said holding my chest.

"What?"

"You can't be scaring people like that."

"Ohhh, why not? It's fun," she said as she lightly punched me in the arm.

"Because I'm on edge."

"What's wrong?" she asked on a more serious note.

"I've been having this weird feeling."

"How so?"

"I think there is another world."

"How do you know?"

"After the last adventure you learn to trust your gut."

By the time lunch came around the power had come back on. I was sitting with Penny. Petey and Mickey were making their way over.

"What's up ladies," Mickey joked as he sat down.

"Oh, nothing new," I said.

Petey came over from the other table he had stopped at and the boys got in the lunch line.

"Aren't we going to tell them?"

"Maybe they can figure it out on their own."

Chapter 2

There were mirrors that surrounded the four of us that showed our past, present, and future. I looked around and I was alone. The maze of mirrors only showed my reflection. All the mirrors accept one.

I woke up in the nurse's office with Penny by my side. "Where are the boys?"

"It's okay. They know."

"But where are they?" The door opened and the two people I was expecting came in.

"Moni, are you okay?" Petey asked.

All I had to do was look at him and he knew. "Should we meet up after school?"

"In the you know where," I said.

"Okay," he said turning to Mickey.

"I'll be there," Mickey said.

"Can you make it through the rest of the day?" Penny asked.

"I hope so," I smiled.

I got back to class and finished off the day. The four of us went to the tree house in Petey's yard. We started research based on my dream. We came to the conclusion that the only place that could have a mirror maze is the amusement park, and it's house of mirrors.

"Okay, so tonight as seven. We will meet by the Ferris wheel," I said going into my bag. "Oh fudge monkeys. I must have left the notes at home."

"Notes of what."

"Well I had a journal started for these visions. I was going to bring them."

"Moni, if they are home, don't worry about it. There's a reason grandma and gramps sent you to live with your brother," Penny said.

"I know, you're right. I should at least try to tell him where I will be."

"No, if he cared, he would call you. He would call your brother. He would call."

"He hasn't called," I said.

Chapter 3

When my brother dropped me off, I told him I would get a ride home from Penny's mom. Mickey was the only one by the Ferris wheel when I got there. "Did they text you?"

"No, they should be here," I said.

"Are you okay?" he asked.

"I had another vision at home. This will not be a fun adventure at all."

"What's going to happen?"

"You have to find out on your own. I can't tell you."

"Why not?"

"Because my vision says I can't." I said sitting down.

"Moni," I heard. I picked my head up I and saw Penny coming over.

"We have to go," I said.

"Petey isn't here yet?"

"So call him," I suggested while holding my head and getting up.

"Petey, where are you?" Mickey asked.

I fell to my knees and was standing in front of a mirror. I took a step closer and put my hand to the glass, but it wasn't glass at all. I walked through my reflection and a yellow flash woke me up. I was in Petey's arms, in the line to the House of Mirrors.

"Look who showed up," I said.

"Are you okay?"

"We have to find the yellow maze."

He put my feet back on the ground. I looked at the ground and became so scared of what my vision may be.

We got to the front of the line and the butterflies in my stomach started to hurt. I tried to smile at the ticket guy as I went by, but I think it came out weird. I went in first and couldn't find the yellow maze.

"Penny, where is the yellow maze?"

"I'm on it right now."

"That doesn't help," I yelled.

I backtracked and was able to find it. I don't know why the four of us split up anyway. I was looking down at the yellow path on the maze floor just to make sure I stayed on the yellow. I was so engrossed in the color that I walked into a mirror and cracked it. I looked at my reflection. *I am broken.*

I kept walking and eventually found Penny. "Where are the boys?"

"They were behind me," I said turning around.

I called Petey, assuming they were together. He told me about a cracked mirror and I told him that he was close. "Is Mickey with you?"

"Yeah, where do we go?" he asked.

"It's easy just stay on the yellow maze and you will get here. Hurry up."

I hung up and looked at Penny.

"Moni, you're breaking a sweat. Sit down."

"Where do you want me to sit," I snapped.

"It doesn't matter," she said soft. "No one else is going to come by."

"Why not?" I asked.

"I think we are the only ones who were invited to this part of the maze."

We waited for the boys, which seemed like forever. When my phone rang I gave it to Penny.

"Ugh, fine. I'll be there in a few minutes." She turned to me and knelt down. "I have to go get them. Stay here, I'll be right back."

She put the phone on the floor and walked between two mirrors. I just sat there, and looked at my different reflections. There was a mirror at the end of the hall that seemed to draw me closer. I got up and stumbled to it. I collapsed to my knees when I was in front of it. "What are you trying to show me?"

The hall went black and I saw mom in the mirror. "Mom."

She didn't say anything back. She just disappeared. I lowered my head and moved back to the wall, and then the lights came back on. I slid down the wall and gently lay on the floor.

"Moni, wake up hun," I heard faintly.

"Mom," I jumped.

"No, it's Penny. Did you see her?"

"I don't know. It felt like a dream."

Petey sat me up and gave me my phone. "So, who's coming with me?"

"Where are we going?" Mickey asked.

"The mirrors. The next world is in the mirrors."

"Why should we go?" Petey asked.

"Right now, I don't know. If I keep seeing my mom, well, I, I can't tell you."

"Why not?"

"It won't let me. That's why I've been passing out so much. I'm seeing what is going to happen."

"So, you can't tell us. You're the only one who knows."

"I know, I just can't. I don't know what would happen to you or me if I tried to tell. Please just trust me on this."

"I don't know if I should," Petey said. "After the last adventure, I think it would be wise to tell us first so we can know what we are up against."

"If I could, I would, but I can't. Please just trust me," I said looking to Penny for some help.

"Petey, think of it this way. Did we know what we were up against last time? We didn't have any idea what we were going into. When I pushed Moni out of the way of that hand I wasn't thinking about where I would end up, but it didn't matter, because I am here now. It has become our responsibility to find out these worlds."

He slowly got up, and disappeared behind the mirror wall. Penny got up without looking at me and slipped behind the wall too. I moved to the wall and could hear Penny quietly trying to persuade him to come.

"I'm not doing this again," he said. "If she is seeing someone she lost years ago, then what am I going to see?"

"Moni," Mickey said touching my shoulder. I wiped my tears away and looked at him.

"It just hurts, the fact that he trusted me before and doesn't trust me now, and it includes my mom this time. It just hurts.

The lights went out and I grabbed Mickey's arm. A spot light came on over me and I looked to the mirror and she was there, looking down at me. I slowly stood up and walked towards the mirror with my hand out. I put my hand to the mirror and it was still solid. The lights came back on as I once again fell to my hands and knees.

"I don't know how to get through."

"She didn't tell you?"

"No, she comes to see me and leaves."

"So, is it a new world?"

"Maybe it's not?"

Chapter 4

"I can't do this."

"Petey, listen. You won't be alone. The three of us have to go through the same thing. We are in this together, just like last time."

"It's nothing against her, just that when she told us that she saw her mom, I got upset because of what I might see. I might see my mom and my dad. The day I lost them. I don't know if I am strong enough to see the accident."

"Give her a chance. You know she would tell you if she could."

I heard a silence and crawled back over to Mickey. No one came back through the wall.

"Do you think they lost the path?" I asked.

"They have only been gone for a few minutes," he said. "You okay?"

"Do I seem okay," I shot back.

"No," he said.

"Then no, I am not okay."

"What's wrong?"

"I have friends that won't back me up."

"That's just Petey. You should know him by now. He's not into this whole superstition thing."

"I would think he would be after our last adventure."

"It takes a lot to persuade him. That's why Penny is the only person who can talk to him when he is like this."

"Our first adventure wasn't enough to persuade him?"

"Well, it seems to me that each world is different. Maybe he is afraid of what will happen."

"Or, what he might see," I said under my breath.

I laid my head on Mickey's shoulder and slowly went to sleep. I was in my house, but it wasn't neat and clean the way mom kept it. The house seemed abandoned even though three people still lived there. I looked to the stairs and was then standing outside a cracked door. Just beyond the door was a crib and the sound of my favorite lullaby. I opened the door and the room flooded with light. The crib disappeared and my worst nightmare was starring back at me.

I woke with a jump on Mickey's lap. He looked down at me with worried eyes.

"Are Petey and Penny back yet?"

"No, not yet. What was that?" he asked.

"What?"

"Your nightmare?"

"Yeah, my nightmare," I said looking away from him.

"Should we call one of them?"

"Maybe we should," I said.

He got his phone out and tried Petey's phone first and got no answer. He gave me the phone and I called Penny.

"Where are you guys?"

"Petey isn't coming. I'm sitting just beyond the mirror that divides us."

"Come talk to us."

She came through the opening and I hung up the phone. "What happened?"

"He's not coming."

"What did he say?"

"It's a waste of time."

"Facing our fears is a waste of time?"

"To him yes," Penny said.

"Let me try to talk to him. Mickey can I have your phone?"

I blocked Mickey's number and could hear the ring on the other end.

Chapter 5

I was able to get him back. It took a while, but he made it back. As soon as he walked through our little doorway I slowly stood up and gave him a hug. "It's okay, you're not alone in this."

The four of us sat against the mirror walls, while I was trying to figure out what was going on. Why would I see the vision that tells me I can go through the mirror, then not be able to in real life? The lights went out and the spot light came on lighting up the mirror. The mirror started to glow and sparkle.

"Come with me," she said.

"It's her," I whispered. "We need to go," I said a little louder.

The four of us held hands and walked into the mirror. A very bright flash welcomed us.

I opened my eyes and was still seeing colored dots. "Penny?"

"Moni, where are you?"

"Penny, I'm right her."

I found her hand and looked to her through colored dots. "Where are we?"

"In the mirror," she said.

My vision started to come back and I saw it was only her and me. "Where are the boys?"

"There is no phone service here," she said.

"Dude, we are in a mirror. Maybe we should suggest that they get phone reception. We are where memories come to life. That's why I saw my mom."

I felt a sharp pain in my head. "You can't tell them. They have to find out on their own."

"I didn't tell them anything."

"Don't tell them," she begged.

"I'm sorry."

"Come on Moni, get up," Penny said.

"It's always me. Don't you see it?"

"I don't see anything but you Moni."

"It's mental Penny. You have a memory. A very powerful memory, much like the one I have. It'll be put to good use tonight."

"Maybe we should try to find Mickey and Petey."

"Okay," I said as she grabbed my hand.

The surroundings were jet black with a faded yellow path at our feet. It was the same yellow color as the floor in the mirror maze.

We followed the path for a long while until we came to a door. It was a brown door. It looked a lot like my bedroom door. Penny reached for the knob, but I stopped her. I reached for the knob and slowly opened the door. It was my room when I was a baby. The room was dark but my crib remained a stark white. I let go of Penny's hand and walked closer to my crib. I was in the crib, awake, looking at the ceiling. I heard the door open and mom come in. It was so good to see her face again. She picked me up from the crib and I could almost feel her arms around me. A tear fell from my eyes and dripped off my chin, onto the floor. I looked down and the floor rippled like water until the vision went away. The yellow path re-appeared at our feet and all we could do was follow it.

Chapter 6

Penny and I came to a wall of mirrors. She stood in front of one, and I in front of another. I felt her handgrip tighter around mine.

"Penny?"

"Moni, you were right. I do have a memory."

A light came on above us, and I smiled and looked at Penny. "You did it." Her legs collapsed beneath her. It was my fastest reaction to catch her.

"Moni, Penny," I heard in the distance.

"Petey," I yelled, but got not response back. I looked down at Penny and smiled as tears started coming. They were happy tears that she finally found herself. Her memory. The memory that has haunting her for years.

"Moni," she said low.

"You did it Penny.'

"I know, thanks."

I looked at the wall of mirrors that stretched in both directions. "How do we get around this?"

"Moni, Penny," I heard a little closer.

"Petey," I yelled louder, but again got no response.

"There is no one here but you and Penny," her voice said.

"Where are the boys?" I asked her.

"Their memories are different than you and Penny, so they are in a different part of this world."

"How can you see them?"

"I'm not alive. When you become a memory you can see things you can't see when you are mortal."

"Will I ever hold your hand again?"

"Yes you will hun. I promise you."

"How am I going to do that?"

"You will find a way," she said starting to fade away.

I looked down at Penny and sat her up. "Do you keep hearing Petey?"

"No."

I looked up at the wall. We can't go any further."

"Why not?" Penny asked.

"Our memories are in the way," I said.

"We have to find the boys," Penny said.

"They aren't here. Well not here, here. They are in a different part of the world. We won't be able to find them."

We both stood up and looked around. There was black nothingness behind us, two mirrors in front of us and dim lit line of mirrors that divided us from the other side.

"What if we find a broken mirror and go through it."

"Penny, do you not understand?"

"Apparently I don't. Understand what?" she asked starting to get aggravated.

"Why we are here. We have four memories that need to disappear from our past. We are here so we can confront them. If we try to avoid them, what would happen to us?"

"Stop being so paranoid. Nothing will happen. We just need to find the boys."

She walked away and turned her attention to possibly a broken mirror. "Moni, come here."

I went over and she pointed to a broken mirror. The glass laid beneath the mirror's frame. "Let's go."

"Don't let her go," I heard mom say.

"Penny, this is someone else's memory. They have beaten theirs. It's time for us to just . . . STOP! Be patient."

"I have been patient for ten years. My problem shows up on my doorstep and you're telling me to wait longer. No, I'm going." She put her foot through and was standing on the other side. She looked back at me. "Nothing happened, now come on."

"No, please come back here," I said worried.

"Really, nothing happened. Moni, stop being so stubborn."

"Penny," I said, "I am not being stubborn. You can't hear your brother talking to you?"

"Wow, are you serious. No, I can't hear him. He's dead."

She fell to her knees, and then dropped to her hands. She looked to me and started to crawl forward.

"Penny, you can't come back. It won't let you. I'm sorry."

She fell to her stomach and rolled to her back. I looked up. "Mom I tried. What's going to happen to her?"

I got no response. I sat against the mirrors and held my knees. I never knew my memories could be this scary, this alone.

Chapter 7

"Moni."

I looked through the broken mirror and Penny was awake. "Can I come back?"

"No, I told you before you passed out. I told you not to go," I said looking down.

"I'm sorry. I'm the risk taker. You should know that by now."

"You've already put your life at risk for me. I won't let you put your life at risk for something that is a part of you," I teared.

"I don't want to face this. This memory. I don't want to relive it."

"You're not facing it alone. You have me and I have you. I'm facing one just like yours. You aren't alone Penny."

"How do we find them? How do we get rid of them?"

"I don't know yet. Maybe if we relive them, they won't hurt as much. We were young when they happened. We will understand why they happened and how they made us stronger."

The line of mirrors started breaking, but stopped when they got to the two center ones. The spotlights above us were now the only lights to break the darkness.

"Penny?"

"I see it."

The mirror I wasn't using flipped over so Penny could see her reflection. "Now what?"

"I guess we wait," I said.

It felt like forever until something happened. I saw Penny's mirror starting to glow. It glowed like the one in the house of mirrors.

"Penny," I said.

I didn't get a response back. That's when I knew her brother had found her. She was now in the mirror reliving her worst nightmare. I hope my turn will be sometime soon. I looked at the mirror that reflected the dark and my face. "Mom, I can only wait for so long. Where are you?"

I still got nothing.

"Okay, I'll wait."

My mirror started to glow, and mom appeared in the mirror. She reached her hand out of the mirror. Her hand was translucent, but I was able to grab it with my living hand. Her hand was still as soft as I remember. She pulled me to my feet and guided me to her world. I put one foot in the mirror and closed my eyes as I walked in.

Chapter 8

There were sirens with police cars and an ambulance outside of our house. The memory was starting to come back. It started to hurt. Mom was standing next to me, and she was solid, instead of a ghost. I put my hand in hers and could finally feel her hands after so long. I heard voices talk in a frantic tone. Strange men ran into our house with red bags.

"I don't remember what happened."

"It's okay. That's why you are here; you're here to relive the worst part of your past. It's okay to be scared, but be brave too."

The picture in front of us sped up until I was standing at the front door. I looked back to mom, and then opened the door. The house was a wreck. The furniture was gone and a layer of mess hid the floor. I heard a bang from the kitchen and slowly walked to the doorway. It was dad. I was sitting in my high chair. He didn't look the way I remembered.

"This was my fault," he said, "if only I loved her more. I knew I shouldn't have taken that job. Now she is slowly being taken from me."

I walked to the sink next to him. "Dad, it's not your fault. None of us saw this coming. You can't blame yourself. I won't let you. I will come back to help you, to help us both understand. Please, just wait."

I turned back to mom, then back to dad and I tried to touch his shoulder, but couldn't, and went back to mom. "I'm ready."

"Maybe I shouldn't show you. I always told you I would protect you from all your fears," she said.

"This is a fear I need to face. You said for me to be free of this memory, I have to overcome it," I said.

We slowly made our way up the steps and I could hear dad behind us. He stumbled up the stairs, ripping on each one. He had a glass bottle in his hand. I stopped on a step and went down to him. He lifted his head to see how many steps he had left. I wanted to help him, but I couldn't. I looked up to mom to see if she could do anything. She disappeared and dad became aware. I heard an angel's voice and slowly stood up. It was mom's voice. I looked down at dad, and knew that he had heard it too. He slowly got back to his feet with the help of the railing, and stumbled up the stairs. I stayed behind him even though I wouldn't be able to catch him.

When we got to the top of the stairs, mom reappeared beside me. "He heard you? Did he hear you that same moment all those years ago?"

"No he didn't, but my mom came to me when I was laying in bed, before my passing. She was keeping me updated on how your dad was doing. Moni, your dad is in a depression that you need to get him out of. I'll help out as much as I can, but you need to help him. I just wish I had given you a sister. You seem so alone."

"No, I have Penny. She's the sister I never had. I'm fine. I will admit, I do get depressed, but I know that is okay."

"Yes it is Moni," she said touching my head.

Dad was standing at the door that led to the bedroom. Her bedroom. The bedroom he has been avoiding for ten years. He slowly opened the door and walked in, leaving it cracked behind him. I walked to the door and peeked inside. I felt a hand on my shoulder and looked up to her.

"It's your turn, but I can't make you take that first step. You have to do that on your own."

Chapter 9

I pushed the door open. The two men with red bags were on either side of mom, and there was a nurse giving her an IV. I stayed by the door because I was in shock to see such a strong woman look so weak.

Once the room calmed down I walked over to the foot of the bed. Dad was kneeling down next to the bed, holding her hand. She looked so pale. She slowly opened her eyes and looked at dad.

"Where's Moni?" she asked weakly.

"She's downstairs in her high chair."

"Bring her in please."

Dad kissed her hand and walked out.

"I am here mom," I said putting my hand on the footboard.

I got on the bed and wanted to stroke her hair and face, but I couldn't. I wasn't real.

The bedroom door opened and dad came in carrying me. I had my head on his shoulder, with my face in his neck. He rubbed my back and put me on the bed. The he touched her hand and she opened her eyes. I crawled up to her head and looked confused. I didn't know why she looked the way she did. Sitting here right now I still don't know what was wrong.

"Mom, what was wrong? You never told me."

"I got really sick. I thought it was just a cold that wouldn't go away. It was a continuous headache that never went away. It kept getting worse."

"So, you kept pushing. You kept living the hard life."

"It's a mom thing."

"So what was wrong?" I asked again.

"I had a tumor. The bigger it grew, the harder it was for me to be mom.

"Where was it?"

"Brain tumor.

"Was it just a tumor?"

"No," she started tearing. "The tumor was cancerous. I'm sorry I wasn't strong enough to beat it."

"Mom, I know you're a mom and you can do pretty much anything, but your not super woman. You did what you could, and I do understand. You were hurting and it would have been selfish if I had asked you to stay."

She knelt down to my level and hugged me. She picked me up and I realized that I had just faced part one of my nightmare. Part one was for me to understand. It's part two that I am scared of. "Can I ask, can I stay until, well, you know?"

"If it will make you feel better," she said.

She put me down and I went back over to the bed.

"What's wrong with mommy?" little me asked daddy. Dad didn't say anything. He picked me up and we slowly walked out. I looked at mom in the bed over his shoulder.

The room was now quiet. The nurse gave mom another IV. I walked closer to the nurse and looked at mom by the doorway.

"Can I touch your hand?"

"You won't be able to hold the hand. You're not real. You're a ghost in this world. Your hand would go through hers."

"Then can I come over and hold yours. It's the same hand," I smiled.

I heard dad's voice downstairs. I left the bedroom and stood at the top of the stairs. Grandma and grandpa were here.

"How she doing?" grandpa asked.

"She'd be very lucky to make it through the night. If you want to go upstairs," he said turning to the side to let them go first.

"Where is Moni?" grandma asked.

"She should be in her room. I gave her blocks to play with."

The three of them started up the stairs. I stood off to the side and watched as dad and grandpa walked to mom's room and grandma went to my room. I was starting to remember bits and piece of the memory. I followed grandma. I stood back and watched as she opened my door. I walked closer and saw little me lift her arms up and grandma pick her up. Little me picked up the blocks and started to hand them to grandma. Grandma sat down on the floor and started spelling something. When she finished it was mom's name. She then stood up and picked me up, turned the lights off and sat in the rocking chair. I could hear my favorite lullaby playing and grandma was singing to me. I walked into the room and sat in front of the crib. I watched as my beautiful memory came to life.

Chapter 10

She gently laid me in the crib. "I don't think you will ever know how good of a mom your mom was."

"I think I do," I whispered.

I went back to mom's room and dad was again kneeling at the side of the bed, and grandpa had his hands on dad's shoulder. I climbed onto the bed next to her. The door slowly opened and grandma came in. She sat on the bed next to dad. Mom's eyes opened but there wasn't a twinkle in them.

"Sandie, it's mom."

"Where's Moni?"

"She's in bed," grandma said.

"I want to hold her one last time.

"You can't give up," dad said, "not yet. I'm not ready."

Mom put her hand on dad's cheek. "God is asking for me. I am ready. You have to be strong for our daughter."

"You only knew here for four years. How will I be able to raise her? She is going to need a mom."

"You will figure it out babe. You will have the two people behind you to help out. Please, go get Moni," she said softly.

Grandma left and came back with me in the blink of an eye. She laid me down next to mom. I was still asleep. Mom brushed hair away from my face and smiled. I could see tears in her eyes.

"I'm going to miss you so much," she said lightly holding my hand. "I wish I could have know you longer, but life has told me this is the end of my mortal life. It is only the beginning for you my dear. Whatever you do you have to promise me something."

The room became still. Mom became still. Her body relaxed and her eyes starred down at me. Her pointer finger was still in my hand. Her other arm with the IV in it was under my head. I saw her tummy stop trying as she went into the kind of sleep that cannot be disturbed.

Grandpa closed her eyes and the nurse took the IV out of her arm.

"Now I know why it hurts so much. Why it's so hard to let go. I never thought I would be able to remember something so far back. I was asleep next to you when you passed. I didn't even say good-bye." I looked to the door and my mom slowly came in.

"I hope this helps," she said.

"It does. It did. Thank you."

I jumped off the bed and ran to her. I jumped into her arms and the bedroom slowly turned to a cemetery. "I didn't want to bury you mom."

"Neither did you father, but I wanted to be buried. I wanted to become part of the earth."

I watched as her casket was lowered into the dirt walls. If she wanted this, then I knew I couldn't argue.

Once the ceremony was over I stood in front of her grave. It had new dirt where they had covered her up, to keep her warm in the winter and cool in the summer. She put her hand on my shoulder. "There is one more thing I have to do that you won't like."

"I have to ask one more thing. What was that promise?"

"You have to tell dad. He needs to know the real truth of everything. Make him fight for what he loves. Make him realize he has a responsibility to you and to Danny."

"Will you help me?"

"As much as possible," she smiled. "Now give me hug. I have to send you back."

"This will be our last hug."

"For a while, yes."

I wanted the hug to last forever. "How do I go back?"

"Close your eyes and let it go."

"Can I have that hug now?"

She opened her arms and I walked into the warmth of her body. "I love you mom."

"I love you Moni. Just let it go."

I closed my eyes and saw the adventure I just had in reverse. As I got closer to the mirror world the images sped up until everything went black.

I woke up with the wall of mirrors in front of me. I looked to Penny's mirror and it was facing the same way as mine. I got up and stood in front of my mirror.

"You did it," she said, "Now go live your life like it was meant to be."

My mirror cracked and the pieces fell to the ground. I felt accomplished, but I miss her more now then I did before. I went over and looked at Penny's mirror. It was still intact, so she hadn't come out yet. I sat next to her mirror, and waited for her to come back.

Chapter 11

I hadn't realized I had gone to sleep until Penny woke me up. She told me I was having a nightmare.

"We should get out of here," I suggested changing the topic.

"Let's go," she said holding out her hand. She pulled me up and we slowly walked.

"We just have to go back the way we came, and the mirrors will do the rest."

We held hands the whole way. I wasn't going to let her go. We got to one part where the wall was not solid, but it wasn't a mirror either. There were probably different portals. "Which one do we take?"

Penny stopped and closed her eyes. "It's this one."

Are you sure?" I asked.

"Yes she is," I heard mom say.

I followed Penny and stepped into the portal. Once we were in the portal I opened my eyes. It was pretty cool. It looked like a rainbow, abstract world. Penny and I stood in one place and let the mirror take us to wherever we are supposed to go. Then the sensation stopped as the exit to the portal opened. We looked out, and it was the house of mirrors from the carnival. We stepped out and my knees felt weak. I turned around to look at the mirror. As the mirror got back to its regular form I could feel the wood beneath my knees. It felt like it was spinning.

"Just let go," she told me.

"I can't."

"You have to. It's part of the experience. Penny has let hers go. You can do it. You can have any other memory, just not this one."

"It was the last time I saw you though."

"Moni, let it go," she said sounding stern.

"Moni," I heard Penny say. "I know it's hard, but you understand now. There is no further use for the memory."

I closed my eyes and saw her and I hugging. The background was black. She was wearing a long black dress with a gold necklace around her neck from me and her wedding ring from dad.

"Do it for dad." She said.

I let the hug go and felt a connection break free.

I woke up and looked to the mirror. I put my hand to the surface and it was solid. "Are Mickey and Petey back yet?"

"Yeah, they just texted me."

Chapter 12

The carnival was still going. The lights were flashing and the music was starting to blend together.

"What time is it?" I asked.

"Like eleven- thirty."

"That's it. It feels like the night is over."

"So am I calling my mom to pick us up?" Penny asked.

"Yes please."

In the car I laid on Penny's lap, and she looked down at me.

"We did it," I said tired.

"Yes we did. You're exhausted. Go to sleep. I'll wake you when we get to my house."

"I thought I was going to my brother's tonight?"

Moni, you have to help dad, I remember mom saying. "Penny, I have to see my dad. It's something I promised my mom."

"Is it absolutely necessary. He's hurt you once. I am not about to let it happen again."

"So I'll call my brother to make you feel better."

"I'll come in with you until he gets there."

I went to sleep for what felt like seconds. Penny woke me up and I sat up. I looked to a worn down-home exterior. If mom were here it'd be fine, but she's not. I looked to Penny and took a deep breath. Her mom got out of the car and folded the seat up. She helped me out, and then Penny got out.

"Be careful," her mom said while hugging her daughter.

I looked at them as they were embraced and smiled.

"Okay, let's go," Penny said looking to me.

We walked to the door hand-in-hand and I knocked on the door, then walked in. "Dad."

"He's in the living room," I heard mom say.

He was sitting on the couch with a drink in his hand, starring blankly at the television.

"Dad," I said again.

"It's your fault," he said.

"It's no one's fault."

"She got the disease after she gave birth to you," he said shooting me a dirty look. He then got up. I felt Penny grab my wrist.

"Mom? How do I . . ?"

A light brightened the living room as dad came closer. I heard a car engine outside. I heard the door burst open. I closed my eyes, trusting was what about to happen. Then the feeling went away and I opened my eyes. The living room was dark again, and dad was on the ground. He was holding his jaw.

"Ryan," I said pushing him aside. What did you do?"

"Moni, mom left me with a responsibility to protect you," he said.

"Yeah, from weirdoes. He's our father."

"He was our father," Ryan said.

"No, you don't mean that. He's still our dad. He's just hidden right now by depression, and confusion."

"Moni, come on."

I went over to dad and knelt down, "Mom, I need help."

The angel's light came back. I looked down at dad and he opened his eyes. "No one intended for this to happened. God wanted me sooner than we thought. You have to be that dad to step up. You need to stand up and face this. Moni has, Ryan has, now it's your turn."

The light went away and I looked at Ryan. Dad sat up and looked to the ceiling. "Was that real?"

"It felt real, but no. The mind is a powerful thing, if you use it the right way."

"I'm sorry," he said.

"For?"

"For not being the dad I needed to be. The ground slowly crumbled beneath my feet the whole time she was battling the monster. When she was taken from me, the monster took me too. I just couldn't get back on track."

"And now you have. You understand now. We understand now why she left us. There is no reason to dread on it. It's time for us to now live for her."

I saw Ryan come over and hold out his hand. Dad looked up to him and took hold of his hand. He helped dad up and it was the beginning of a new life, a new life of healing and recovery.

Going to bed that night I felt safe and warm. We were staying with dad. Danny and I shared a bed.

"Have we started on a path to recovery?" I asked him.

"I think we have."

Are there any other worlds that can help us understand who were are as human beings? Will these worlds test our senses and push our minds to the limits? There is only one way to find out.

The adventures continue in

Apart from Our

Own

The "Healers"

www.ingramcontent.com/pod-product-compliance
Lightning Source LLC
Chambersburg PA
CBHW050908120626
46554CB00003B/1077